Santa Monica Public Library
I SMP 00 2717280 Y

S0-CFO-947

EXPLORE my world

Coral Reefs

Jill Esbaum

NATIONAL GEOGRAPHIC KiDS

WASHINGTON, D.C.

A coral reef!

Beneath sparkling ocean waves, sunbeams shine on a world of strange shapes and brilliant colors.

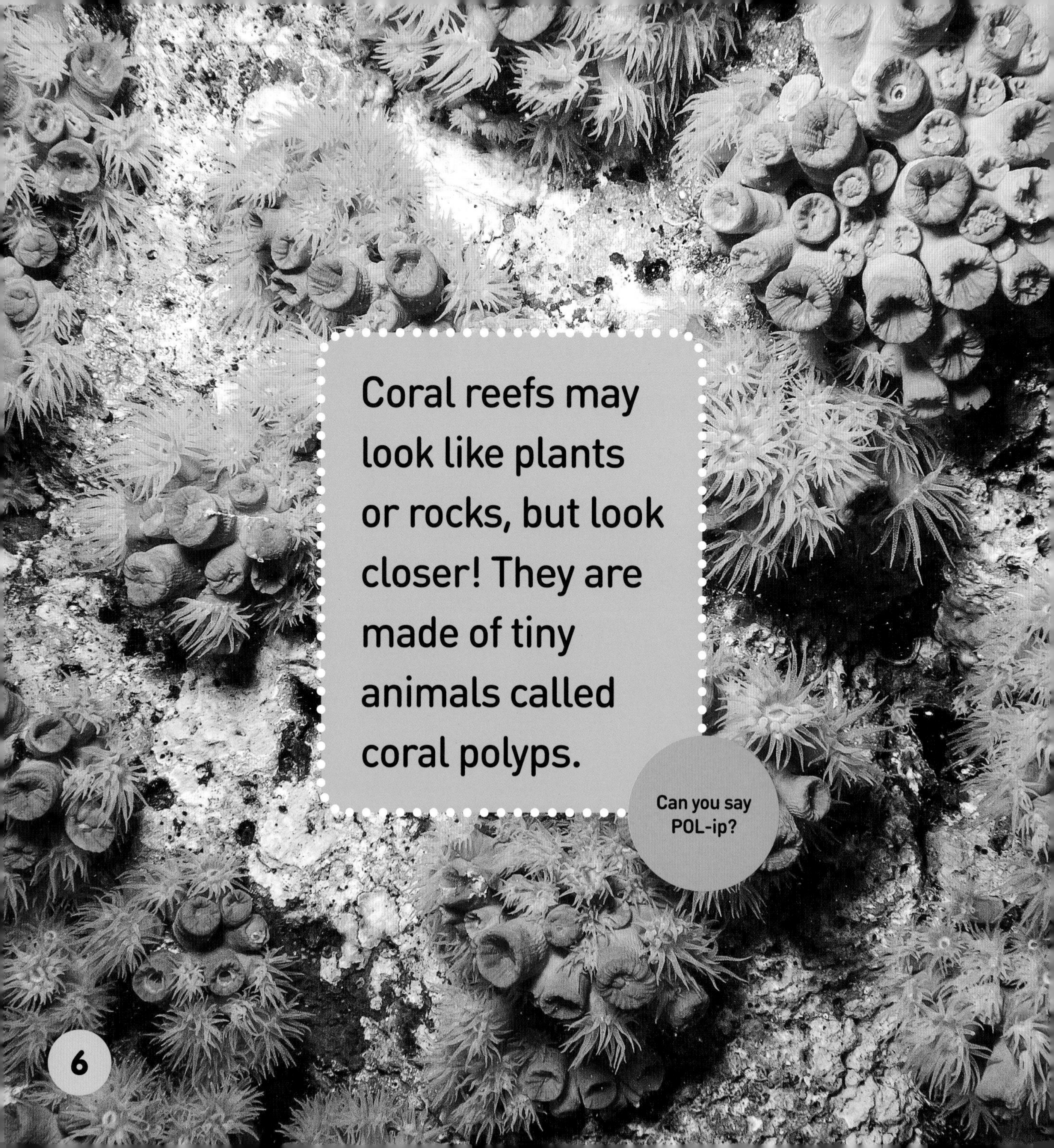

Coral reefs may look like plants or rocks, but look closer! They are made of tiny animals called coral polyps.

Can you say POL-ip?

This photo is a close-up. In real life, a coral polyp is no bigger than a pencil eraser.

Each coral polyp builds a hard skeleton around its soft body. As new polyps build on top of old ones, a coral reef slowly grows.

Shimmer!

A coral reef is a busy place, teeming with creatures big and small.

Some are in a hurry. Schools of colorful fish dart to and fro. Swim this way! No, wait. That way!

Some animals take their time. Parrotfish dawdle along, biting off bits of reef.

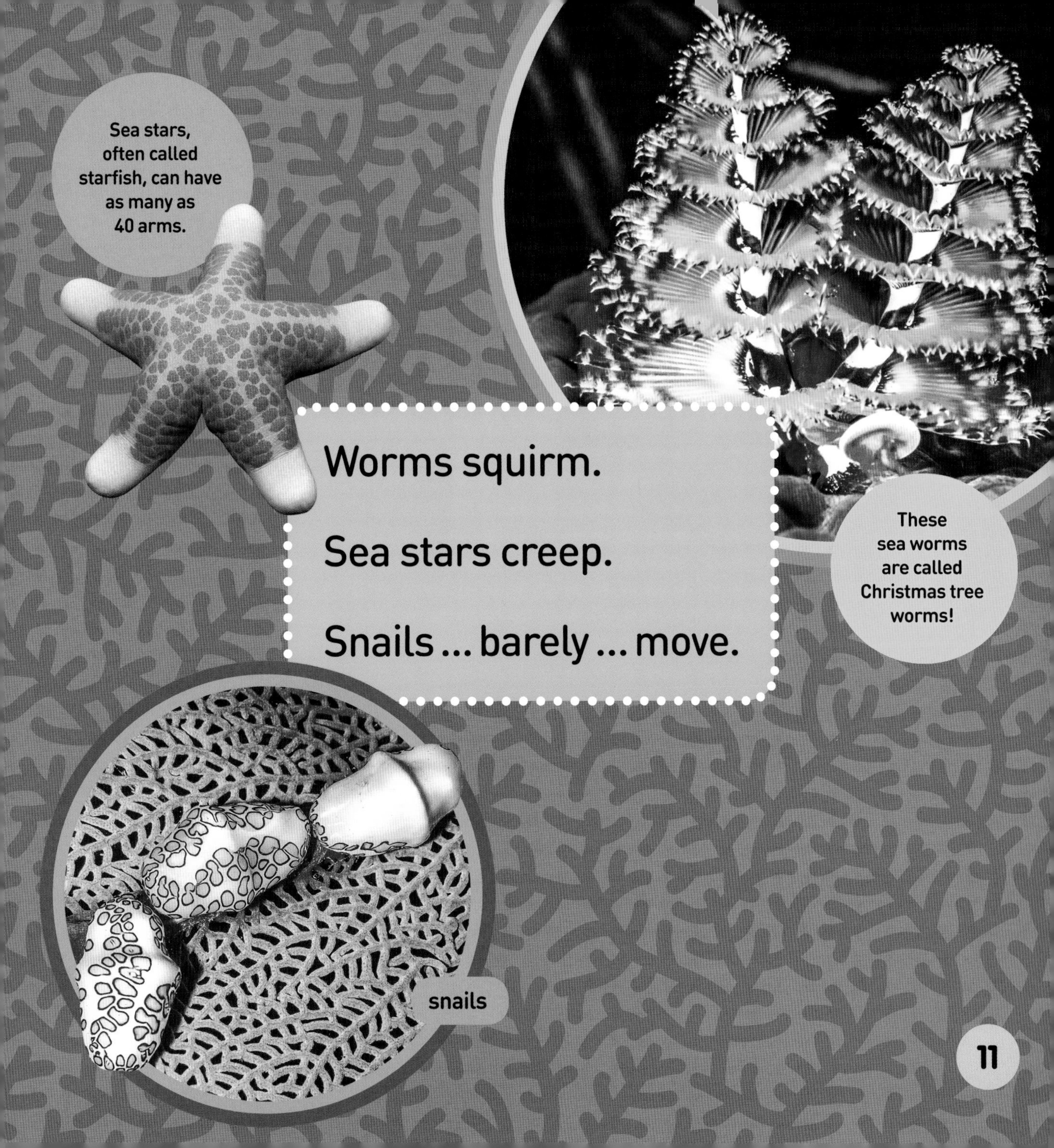

Worms squirm.

Sea stars creep.

Snails ... barely ... move.

Chomp!

An eel lunges from a crack in the coral, just missing a lucky fish.

An octopus scrunches into a cozy cave.

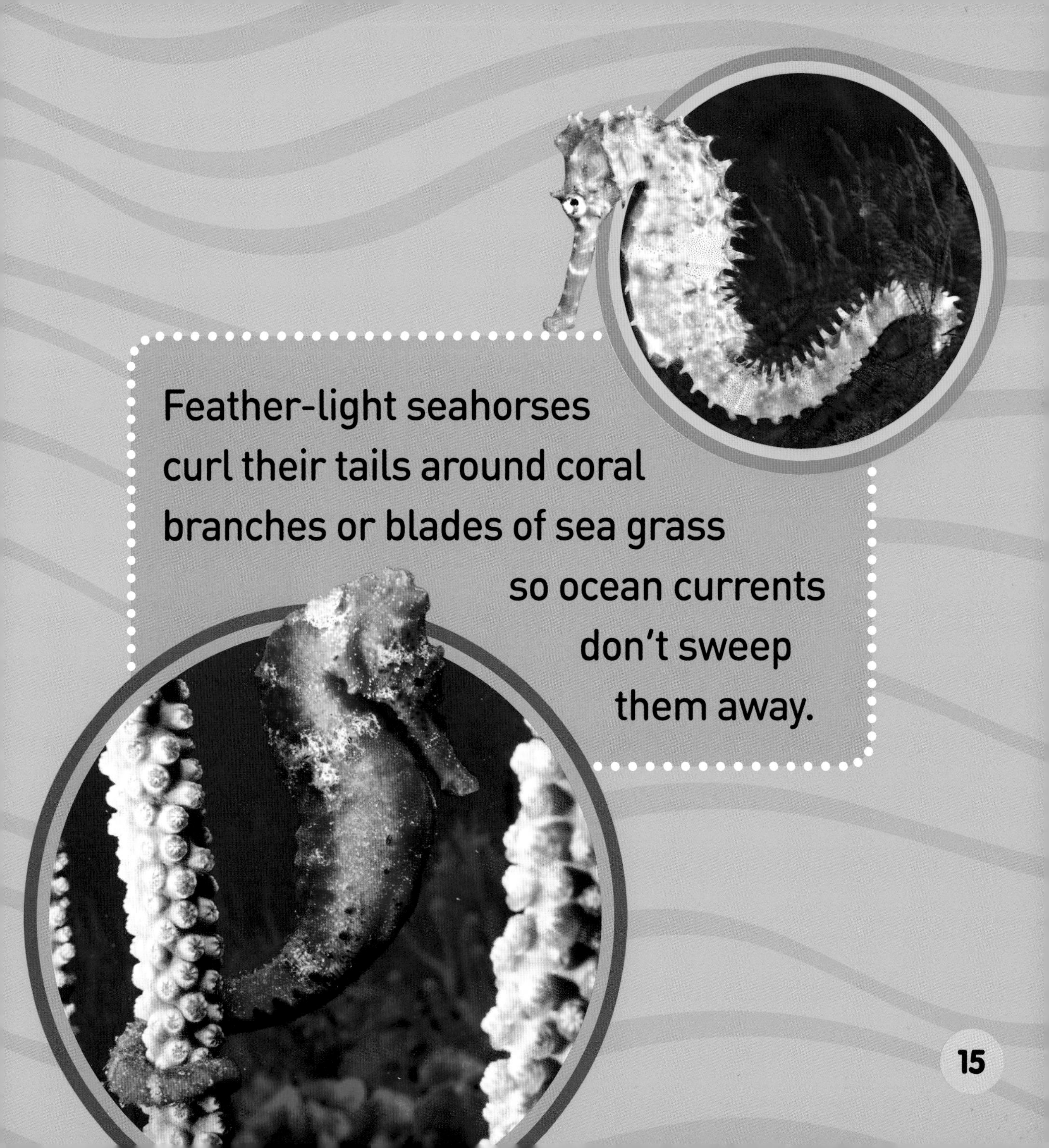

Feather-light seahorses curl their tails around coral branches or blades of sea grass so ocean currents don't sweep them away.

Sand dollars stay in place by digging in.

Spiky sea urchins can hold on anywhere.

Sitting in one spot all its life gives a giant clam plenty of time to eat—and GROW.

Hello, there!

A clownfish peeks through the swaying tentacles of a sea anemone.

Sea anemones look like flowers, but they are animals. Can you say uh-NEM-uh-nees?

A sea turtle snacks on sea grass.

Sneak . . .

After dark, rays and sharks and other sneaky night hunters slip in and out of the moon's shadows. Watch out, little fishes!

An eel waits patiently as its dinner swims closer.

An octopus stretches its arms out to feel for food.

A squirrelfish searches for shrimp.

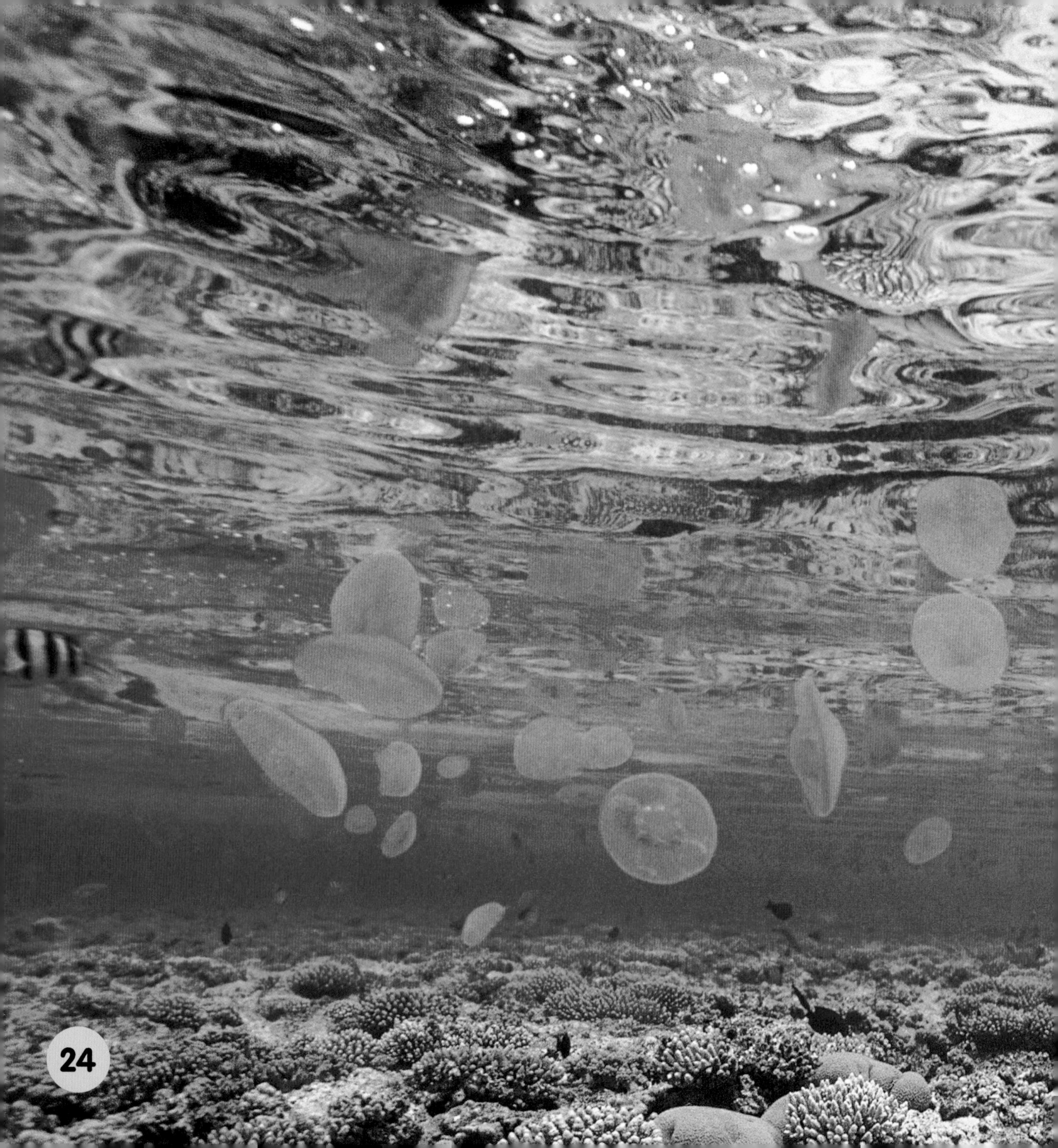

Wake up, coral reef!

Beneath sparkling ocean waves, shimmering fish dart to and fro ...

... as jellyfish drift into a new day.

What's for Dinner?

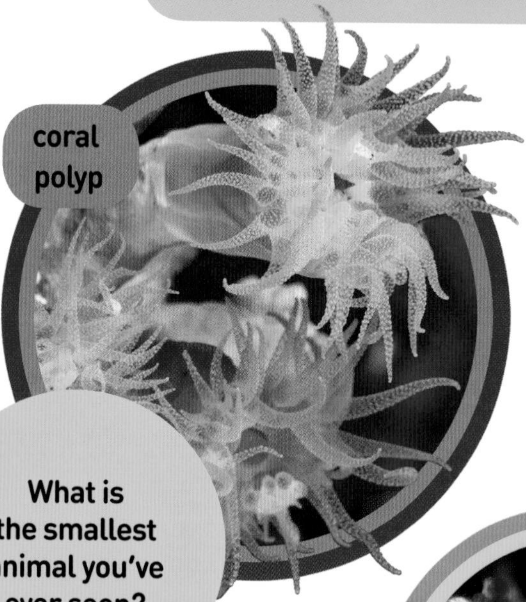

sea worm

coral polyp

A coral polyp eats newly hatched crabs, fish, shrimp, and sea worms. It uses the tentacles around its mouth to sting and capture the teeny creatures.

What is the smallest animal you've ever seen?

crab

Corals also get eaten. Animals such as sea stars, parrotfish, and butterflyfish all nibble on corals.

Cool Corals!

toadstool mushroom leather coral

What colors do you see in this coral reef?

There are hundreds of different kinds of corals in Earth's oceans. They come in a rainbow of colors. Some corals grow into amazing shapes. They can look like antlers, spiky fingers, or even brains! Here are just a few.

staghorn coral

brain coral

Can you draw a colorful coral reef?

sea fans

elkhorn coral

How many different corals can you count on these two pages?

Earth's Coral Reefs

This map shows where coral reefs are found around the world.

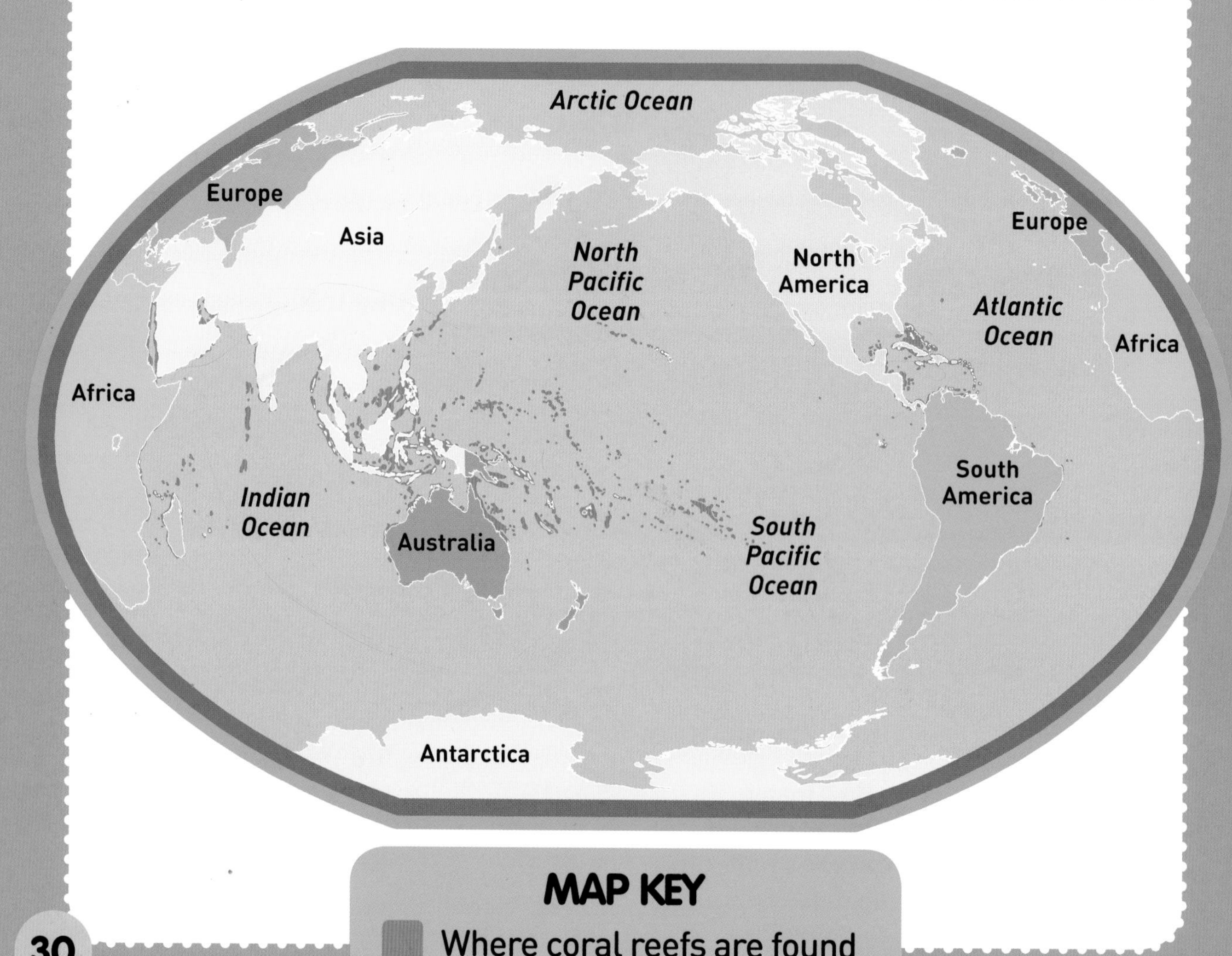

MAP KEY

Where coral reefs are found

Hide-and-Seek

Many creatures that live in coral reefs are good at hiding in plain sight. Can you find the animal in each picture?

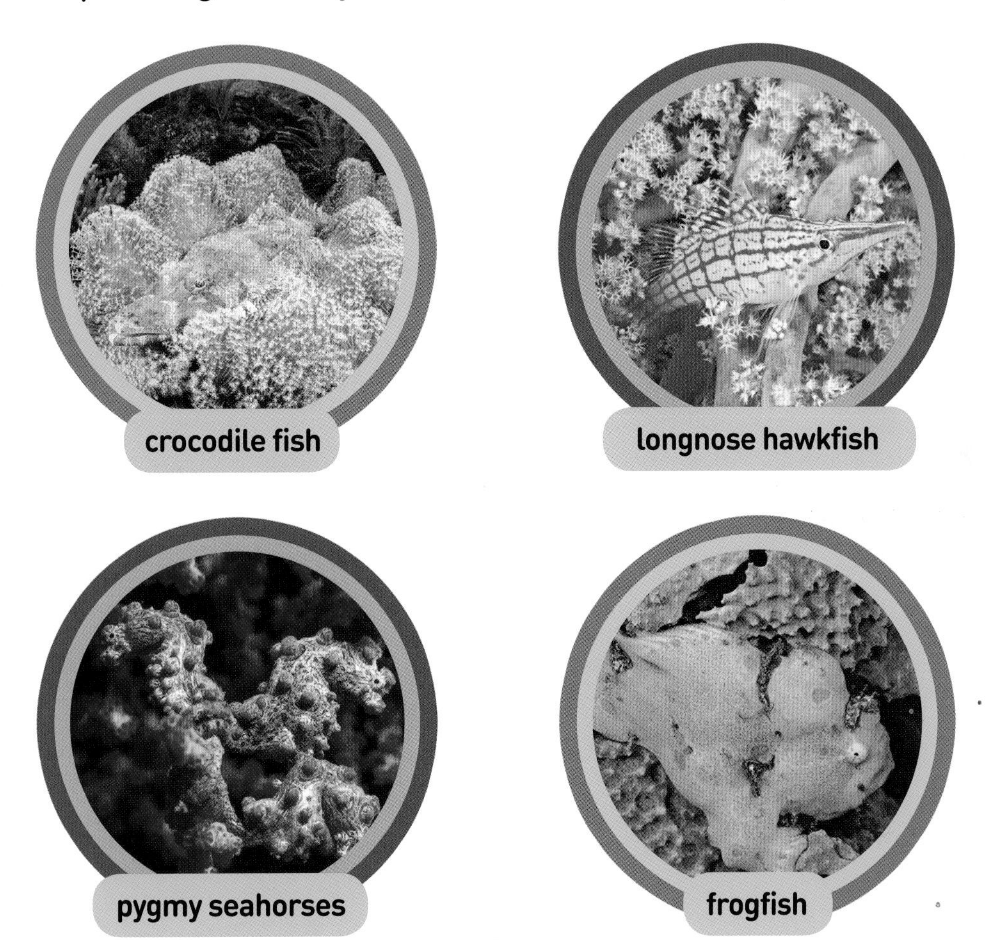

crocodile fish

longnose hawkfish

pygmy seahorses

frogfish

For Maverick —J. E.

Since 1888, the National Geographic Society has funded more than 12,000 research, exploration, and preservation projects around the world. The Society receives funds from National Geographic Partners, LLC, funded in part by your purchase. A portion of the proceeds from this book supports this vital work. To learn more, visit natgeo.com/info.

NATIONAL GEOGRAPHIC and Yellow Border Design are trademarks of the National Geographic Society, used under license.

Library of Congress Cataloging-in-Publication Data

Names: Esbaum, Jill, author.
Title: Explore my world : coral reefs / by Jill Esbaum.
Other titles: Explore my world.
Description: Washington, DC : National Geographic Kids, [2018] | Series: Explore My World | Audience: Ages: 3-7. | Audience: Grades: K to Grade 3.
Identifiers: LCCN 2017020432| ISBN 9781426329852 (paperback) | ISBN 9781426329869 (hardcover)
Subjects: LCSH: Coral reefs and islands--Juvenile literature.
Classification: LCC GB461 .E73 2018 | DDC 551.42/4--dc23
LC record available at https://lccn.loc.gov/2017020432

The publisher gratefully acknowledges Dr. Danielle Dixson, School of Marine Science and Policy, University of Delaware, for her expert review of this book. Thanks also to early childhood development specialist Dr. Marc H. Bornstein, editor, *Parenting: Science and Practice*.

Designed by Brett Challos

Printed in Hong Kong
17/THK/1

ILLUSTRATIONS CREDITS
GI = Getty Images, NG = National Geographic Creative, SS = Shutterstock

Front cover, Georgette Douwma/GI; back cover, richcarey/GI; 1, richcarey/GI; 2–3, PBorowka/GI; 4–5, mihtiander/GI; 6–7, johnandersonphoto/GI; 8–9, Enric Sala/NG; 10, richcarey/GI; 11 (UP LE), Frank & Joyce Burek/NG; 11 (UP RT & LO), johnandersonphoto/GI; 12 (LE), Richard Whitcombe/SS; 12 (RT), Yann hubert/SS; 13, WhitcombeRD/GI; 14, Borut Furlan/GI; 15 (UP), Alex Mustard/ Minden Pictures; 15 (LO), Dickson Images/GI; 16 (UP), Jak Wonderly; 16 (LO), NatalieJean/SS; 17, Alex Mustard/ Minden Pictures; 18–19, Aleksey Stemmer/SS; 19, hocus-focus/GI; 20, Brian J. Skerry/NG; 21, serg_dibrova/SS; 22–23, Reinhard Dirscherl/GI; 23 (UP), ShaneGross/GI; 23 (LO), robertdewit66/GI; 24–25, Frederic Pacorel/GI; 26 (UP), Jad Davenport/NG; 26 (CTR), Howard Chew/Alamy Stock Photo; 26 (LO), David Fleetham/Alamy Stock Photo; 27 (UP LE), tae208/GI; 27 (UP RT), Krzysztof Odziomek/SS; 27 (LO), Global_Pics/GI; 28 (LE), Design Pics Inc/NG; 28 (RT), Hamizan Yusof/SS; 29 (UP LE), Matt Propert/NG; 29 (UP RT), johnandersonphoto/GI; 29 (LO LE), Stocktrek Images/NG; 29 (LO RT), John A. Anderson/SS; 30 (map data), UNEP-WCMC, Worldfish Centre, World Resources Institute, The Nature Conservancy; 31 (UP LE), Alex Mustard/ Minden Pictures; 31 (UP RT), Tim Laman/NG; 31 (LO LE), Sidney Smith/NiS/Minden Pictures; 31 (LO RT), Birgitte Wilms/ Minden Pictures; 32, Isabelle Kuehn/SS; fan coral background, stuckmotion/SS; small coral background, ratselmeister/SS

If you visit a coral reef, enjoy it with your eyes only. Be careful not to touch it or step on it. Thousands of different kinds of creatures depend on coral reefs for food and shelter. That's why it's important to protect coral reefs and help keep them healthy.